That's Not Dasher That's My Dog!

by Adalyn & McKenna Vidoni
Illustrated by Daniel Tompkins

It was Christmas Eve in a small New York town and they were expecting a huge snowstorm. Addie and Kenna were getting really excited for the snow and Santa to come. The fire was crackling, the Christmas tree sparkling and the house smelled like cinnamon and candy canes.

To prepare for Santa, the whole family was cooking, a Christmas tradition. Mom was making chocolate peanut clusters. Dad was making pepperoni rolls. Addie and Kenna were making reindeer food using a special family recipe, which they followed step by step. Their dogs Bronxie and Brookie watched closely in hopes that a piece of food would drop to the floor.

Meanwhile, Santa and his reindeer were making their way through the storm to make sure they could deliver all of the presents on time. Santa was worried that the snow would slow them down and also noticed that his reindeer were having a hard time keeping up their energy.

To help his reindeer, Santa would let each one take a quick break while he was delivering the presents. First Comet, then Donnor, then Dasher and so on. He was so happy when families left out treats for his reindeer. The reindeer were happy too.

Addie and Kenna were closely tracking Santa to see where he was and when he would get to New York.

It is almost time! They left out cookies and milk for Santa and their special reindeer food for the reindeer. Kenna put reindeer antlers on Brookie, while Addie put a jingle bell collar around her neck so when Santa came, they would hear the bells.

Santa was passing over NYC high above the Empire State building, Rockefeller Center and Radio City Music Hall. He was on his way to upstate NY!

The snow was coming down so heavy, Santa could barely see where he was going. He finally landed on Addie and Kenna's roof. It was Dasher's turn to take a quick break. "Let's go Dasher, everyone is asleep." said Santa.

Santa and Dasher made their way down the chimney, but not everyone was asleep. Brookie was sitting as awake as a doodle could be ready to play. Bronxie, a bit older, was fast asleep. All of a sudden Brookie's bells began to jingle.

Addie and Kenna jumped up out of bed when they heard the jingle bells jingle.

Brookie started jumping around the room. Santa heard a noise coming from upstairs. "Holy Candy Canes" he said, "I need to get out of here before they see me!" A very flustered Santa went to get Dasher, but with all the commotion, accidentally grabbed Brookie's collar instead and whisked her up the chimney.

When they arrived on the roof, Santa quickly hooked up Brookie to the reindeer straps and jumped in the sleigh. Since it was snowing so hard, Santa didn't even notice he put Brookie in Dasher's spot and they flew off into the night.

When Addie and Kenna came downstairs, they noticed that Bronxie was sleeping and Brookie looked a bit different. "That's not Brookie, that's a Reindeer!" they shouted.

With all of the loud racket, Mom and Dad were now up. "What is going on? Addie, Kenna, why is there a reindeer in our living room? Where is Brookie?"

Addie and Kenna looked at each other and shouted, "Santa must have taken Brookie by mistake!"

Meanwhile, Brookie was flying through the air hanging a good six feet lower than the rest of the reindeer. Her tongue was hanging out and she had a smile from one floppy ear to the other.

She was so low, she smacked right through a snowbank leaving a dog imprint in the snow.

Santa finally began to notice something was a bit amiss. "Why is Dasher hanging down so low? Why is my Sleigh oh so slow? What are those white and black markings? What is with the barking?" He said.

Santa decided to take a quick pit stop to check out his team. "Hmmm, Dasher doesn't have brown antlers or furry feet. Dasher isn't poofy or that goofy!" Santa thought for a minute and realized that he must have grabbed the wrong reindeer...or in this case the wrong dog! "That's not Dasher, that's a dog!"

Santa quickly turned the Sleigh around, but had no idea where to go. He couldn't change his GPS as it was already set up with the rest of his route and he was running out of time. "What do I do? " he said.

All of a sudden Brookie caught on to a scent. Was that the smell of peanut clusters? A pepperoni roll? Reindeer food?!? Brookie quickly pointed down below and started to bark as if she had seen a squirrel. "That's it doggy, keep on barking!" said Santa as he steered the sleigh.

All of a sudden the feeling of joy began to put a smile on Santa's face. Below he could hear Addie and Kenna shouting, "That's not Dasher, that's our dog!" Santa began to laugh and he kicked it into high gear towards the house.

Santa parked his sleigh and thanked Addie and Kenna for taking such good care of Dasher. "Animals are very important to us Santa." they said. "Christmas traditions, like cooking with your family, are also very important. Thanks to Brookie's sense of smell and your traditions, we were able to find our way back safely." said Santa. And just like that Santa was gone into the night.

When Addie and Kenna got back inside they noticed Santa left them a bunch of presents. As excited as they were to open them, they realized that the most important thing about Christmas is family and the traditions we share. They hope you enjoy the reindeer food recipe and that you will pass it down from generation to generation, making it a special memory with your family too. Merry Christmas!

Addie and Kenna's Special Reindeer Food Recipe

Ingredients

Big bowl of Popcorn (Homemade or store bought)
1 (12 oz) bag Vanilla Candy Melts
1 1/2 cups or small bag of thin pretzel sticks
1 (10 oz) bag green and red coated chocolate candies
Red and Green sprinkles

Instructions

1. Pour a bag of popcorn into a large bowl. Add in Bag of candy coated chocolates and a small bag of thin pretzel sticks. You can also break pretzel sticks to make smaller pieces.

2. Melt Vanilla Candy Melts in a microwave safe bowl in 20-30 second intervals or a double boiler on the stove until melted and stir until smooth. Drizzle half of melted chips over the popcorn mixture, gently mixing it a few times with a flexible spatula.

3. Then drizzle the remaining half of melted chips over popcorn, and gently stir mixture until evenly coated (make sure you don't over mix, so the white chocolate doesn't harden.)

4. Spread mixture evenly across wax paper on a cookie sheet. Add sprinkles across the mixture evenly to give it some extra Christmas color. Let it cool and harden, then gently break into pieces and store in an airtight container.

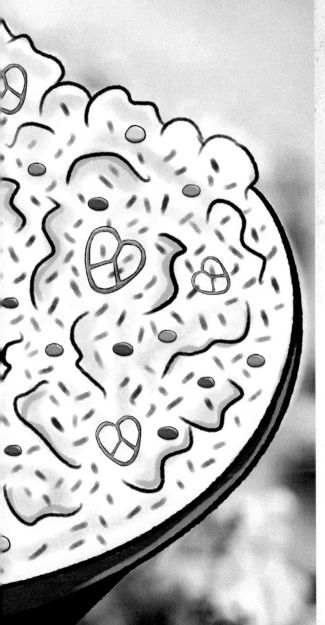

What are your family traditions?

Red velvet Cake

Prime Rib

Peanut Clusters

Pepperoni Roll

Pierogi with Keilbasa

Tomato Pie

Apple Pie

Greens

Reindeer Food

Golabki

Baklava

Recipe Name

Prep Time _____ Cook Time _____

Ingredients

_____   _____

_____   _____

_____   _____

_____   _____

_____   _____

_____   _____

Directions

_____

_____

_____

_____

_____

Recipe Name

Prep Time _____ Cook Time _____

Ingredients

_____   _____

_____   _____

_____   _____

_____   _____

_____   _____

_____   _____

Directions

_____

_____

_____

_____

_____

Recipe Name

Prep Time _____ Cook Time _____

Ingredients

_____   _____

_____   _____

_____   _____

_____   _____

_____   _____

_____   _____

Directions

_____

_____

_____

_____

_____

_____

Recipe Name

Prep Time _____ Cook Time _____

Ingredients

_____   _____

_____   _____

_____   _____

_____   _____

_____   _____

_____   _____

Directions

_____

_____

_____

_____

_____

Recipe Name

Prep Time _____ Cook Time _____

Ingredients

_____   _____

_____   _____

_____   _____

_____   _____

_____   _____

_____   _____

Directions

_____

_____

_____

_____

_____

If you enjoyed this book, you might like our other book,

The House That Gave Out Full Size Candy Bars

Made in United States
Orlando, FL
17 December 2024

56099318R00020